Flash Harriet
and the Missing Ostrich Eggs

Written by Karen Wallace

Illustrated by Andy Rowland

 Collins

1 Ostrich eggs alert

Flash Harriet was reading her favourite book inside her treehouse. It was called *Amazing Agents* and it was written by her Uncle Proudlock, who was the best detective in the world.

A tremendous noise rattled the windows.

CRACK! WHIRR! CLANG!

CRACK! WHIRR! CLANG!

Flash Harriet sighed and put down her book.

Her father, the composer, Norman Brilliant, was practising his new piece of music, *Brilliant Noise*. This one was written for using ostrich eggs, electric whisks and triangles.

While Norman Brilliant banged the piano, the other musicians used one hand to beat the ostrich egg whites with the whisks and bashed their triangles with the other. By the end of the *Noise*, the egg whites were whipped up into a mountain of sticky meringue which covered the entire orchestra. It was a work of genius and everyone hoped it would be a huge success!

Almost everyone.

Flash Harriet's mother, an ex-acrobat called Sequin Cynthia, hated anything sticky so much that she had moved into a tent on the roof.

CRACK! WHIRR! CLANG!

CRACK! WHIRR! CLANG!

Flash Harriet stood up and looked outside. Her mother was doing handsprings on top of the chimney and her face was bright red.

Inside the treehouse, a tarantula called Gus dangled from the ceiling and rolled his eyes. Flash Harriet felt herself smiling. Gus had been her Uncle Proudlock's idea.

"Best guard dog on eight legs," he'd said. And Uncle Proudlock had been absolutely right. No one was as quick and smart as Gus.

An envelope fell
through the letterbox.
It was covered in
white fluff. Flash Harriet
knew it was from
Barnaby Fuddle who
delivered the ostrich
eggs to her father
every morning.
She opened it up.

FLASH HARRIET
DETECTIVE AGENCY
THE TREE HOUSE

"Help!" she read. "Someone is stealing my eggs!
I've got no money left and I'm desperate.
You're the only one who can save me. BF."

Flash Harriet gasped. If Norman Brilliant didn't get his
ostrich eggs, *Brilliant Noise* would have to be cancelled.
Flash Harriet put Gus into his special travelling box
and fixed it to her belt.

"First stop, Fuddle Farm!" she told him. She slid
down the fireman's pole and jumped on to her
motor-powered tricycle.

Flash Harriet was on the case!

6

2 Trouble at Fuddle Farm

"Thank goodness, you're here!" squawked Barnaby Fuddle. Two worried-looking ostriches stood beside him and his face was all blotchy as if he'd been crying. "I don't know what to do!"

Flash Harriet thought quickly.

"Does anyone know?"

"Only the bank manager," replied Barnaby Fuddle. "I borrowed money from him, and as soon as I had no eggs to sell, he asked for the money back."

Barnaby Fuddle threw back his head and howled.

"He's a nasty, shark-faced meanie, and without the money or any eggs to sell, I'm going to have to sell my farm!"

Flash Harriet and Gus exchanged looks. Poor Barnaby Fuddle! He looked as if he hadn't slept for days.

"When did you first notice the eggs were missing?" asked Flash Harriet.

"A couple of months ago," replied Barnaby Fuddle. "But only a few at a time were stolen. Then last week the whole lot were taken every day." He burst into tears. "What am I going to do? All I've got is the farm."

The two ostriches on either side looked as if they were going to burst into tears, too.

"Why don't you have a little lie down?" said Flash Harriet, kindly.

Flash Harriet took out her notebook and pencil. She hadn't been to Fuddle Farm before and didn't want to miss any clues. There were wooden huts for shelter and there were ostriches everywhere. Some of them nibbled at the grass and some of them sat on nests they had scraped out of the ground. But they all had the same puzzled look on their faces.

It was as if they couldn't understand why their eggs kept disappearing.

A yellow car stopped on the road and a large woman jumped out. She had yellow hair and wore baggy white overalls. A bowl of custard made of velvet was sewn across her front and the words *Ostrich Delight* were stitched in gold thread underneath.

"Greta Gloop's the name!" cried the woman, grabbing Flash Harriet by the hand. "I've come to talk to Barnaby Fuddle. Have you seen him about?"

"Why?" asked Flash Harriet.

Greta Gloop grinned a yellow-toothed grin. "I buy eggs from him for my custard factory, and we're selling so much that I want to buy even more eggs from him!"

Flash Harriet thought quickly. Could she trust Greta Gloop? Yes, she thought she could.

Gus rattled the bars of his box. He thought so, too.

That was it. Flash Harriet told Greta Gloop all about how the bank manager was forcing the sale of Fuddle Farm because there were no eggs to sell. And no eggs spelt disaster for her father's *Brilliant Noise*.

"Let's check the nests right away," said Greta Gloop, when she'd heard everything. "If there are new eggs, the thieves will strike again tonight."

They walked around the field and looked inside the nests. Every nest was full of eggs.

There was no time to lose.

"We'll come back to Fuddle Farm tonight," said Flash Harriet. "We can keep watch and catch any thieves red-handed."

"Good idea," replied Greta Gloop.

Flash Harriet sent a text to her mother to let her know what she was doing.

But when they got back to Fuddle Farm that night to tell Barnaby Fuddle about their plans, he was nowhere to be seen.

While they waited, Greta Gloop pulled out two jars of Ostrich Delight. She handed Flash Harriet a spoon.

"Try some."

Flash Harriet swallowed a mouthful.

Greta Gloop was right!

It tasted absolutely delicious!

Flash Harriet and Greta Gloop hid in view of the ostriches, and Flash Harriet peered through her binoculars. All she saw were the shadowy shapes of a few ostriches wandering about.

"Nothing here but ostriches," she sighed.

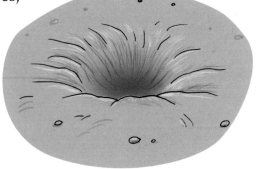

After two hours, they checked the nests.

All the eggs were gone!

Somehow they'd been stolen from right under Flash Harriet and Greta Gloop's noses.

Suddenly, they heard the sound of a car. They peeked out and saw a man standing by a purple limousine. He had a face like a shark with slicked back hair and he was taking pictures of the field.

Flash Harriet's hair stood on end. Everything about this man spelt trouble!

As Flash Harriet walked back to the Fuddle Farm
house with Greta, she took out her phone and
sent Uncle Proudlock a long text. She needed
a breakthrough, and he was the only person in
the world who could help.

3 New developments

If it hadn't been for Gus, Flash Harriet would never have seen the photograph. She was sitting on her tricycle on her way home when suddenly Gus began to jump up and down in his travelling box. A split second later, she turned and found herself staring at a newspaper stand. The man with the shark face was on the front page!

Flash Harriet grabbed a copy of the paper. The man was called Colin Grabbit and he was a property developer who had just opened a new office in the High Street.

Flash Harriet turned her handlebars hard right. It was time to pay Mr Grabbit a visit!

"Can I help you?"
A woman with purple hair sat behind a metal desk, playing games on a computer.

"I want to speak to Colin Grabbit, please," said Flash Harriet.

Before the woman had time to pick up the phone, another door opened.

"Colin Grabbit at your service," said a man wearing a pink shirt.
He was the same man she had seen at Fuddle Farm.

Flash Harriet stared at his nasty shark face and once again felt something niggling at the back of her mind.

23

"I'm looking for a field to build a factory on," she said.

It was the first thing that had come into her mind, but it worked.

"I have exactly what you need." Colin Grabbit rubbed his hands together as if they were covered in soap bubbles. "Best investment you'll ever make. But it won't be available for twenty-four hours."

"Twenty-four hours?" croaked Flash Harriet.

Colin Grabbit scowled.

"What's the problem? Twenty-four hours means tomorrow."

Flash Harriet didn't reply. Things were much worse than she thought. She ran into the street and sent Uncle Proudlock another message.

4 A cunning plan

For the first time since Flash Harriet had set herself up as a detective, she was worried. Her windows rattled as her father banged his piano and the orchestra played *Brilliant Noise*.

Flash Harriet buried her face in her hands. If she didn't solve the case in time, Norman Brilliant's career would be over.

Something fluttered into the room. A carrier pigeon landed with a thud on top of her in-tray. It was from her Uncle Proudlock and it must have hitched a ride on the tail of an aeroplane!

With shaking hands, Flash Harriet opened the message tube.

If a wolf can look like a sheep, a thief can look like an ostrich.

Flash Harriet frowned. What on earth did that mean?

IN

27

She sat down on her chair and read the message again. She had never known Uncle Proudlock to be wrong. Then a wide grin spread across her face. Of course! Why hadn't she worked it out for herself? She picked up the phone and dialled the number for *Freddie's Fancy Dress Company*.

Twenty minutes later a van stopped outside the treehouse.

"You're lucky I had two left," said the driver, as he put down a large box on the office floor. "They've been very popular recently."

Flash Harriet thanked him and ripped open the box. Inside were two feathery costumes. She climbed into one of them and peered in the mirror. She looked just like an ostrich on Barnaby Fuddle's Farm!

No wonder she hadn't noticed anything suspicious last night. The thieves had been wearing ostrich suits!

There was a bang on the door and Greta Gloop burst into the room.

From inside her costume, Flash Harriet saw Greta Gloop's eyes nearly pop out of her head.

"Greta!" cried Flash Harriet, as she pulled the head off her costume. "It's me! I've got a plan!"

"Aaargh!" squawked Greta Gloop. Then she fainted on the floor!

5 Off with their heads!

Greta Gloop gulped her tea.

"And that's when I knew we would both be millionaires,"
she cried. "As soon as he tasted the custard!"
Greta Gloop slammed down her cup and looked tough.
"No shark-faced meanie bank manager is going to get
his mitts on Fuddle Farm. I need those eggs for
my factory!"

Flash Harriet felt her skin prickle. It was a clue, and she
knew it. How many people looked like sharks?
Was it a coincidence that a bank manager and
a property developer had the same kind of face?

"What's the manager's name?" asked Flash Harriet.

"Nigel Grabbit," replied Greta Gloop.

It was as if all the pieces of the jigsaw were beginning to join up! Why would a bank manager and a property developer get together to force Barnaby Fuddle to sell his farm?

So they could make lots of money from it, was the answer.

Only a bank manager could demand his money back, and without any eggs to sell, Barnaby Fuddle had no choice but to sell the farm to get the money. And if Barnaby needed the money quickly, he would agree to selling the farm for a cheaper price. And only a property developer could sell the farm for a higher price and make a lot of money!

But first of all, to make Barnaby desperate enough to sell his farm, they had stolen the eggs.

It was all about making lots of money. And if Flash Harriet was right, it was definitely a matter for the police.

So while Greta tried on her costume, Flash Harriet went outside and made two telephone calls: one to Barnaby Fuddle and the other to the police.

It was almost dark when Flash Harriet, Barnaby
Fuddle and Greta Gloop met at Fuddle Farm.
Flash Harriet and Greta Gloop were both dressed up
as ostriches and Flash Harriet was carrying
a camera. She had told Greta it was her job to identify
the thieves and pull off the heads of their costumes.
Then she would shine a torch on their faces and take
a photograph, while Barnaby turned on the spotlight
above them.

"How will I tell a real ostrich from a fake one?"
asked Greta Gloop, as they climbed over a fence into
the field.

"Raisins," replied Flash Harriet. "Ostriches love them. If you meet an ostrich who isn't interested, you'll know it's a fake."

"Which means it's a thief dressed up as an ostrich," said Greta Gloop.

"Exactly," said Flash Harriet.

The moon came out from behind a cloud.

Several ostriches were moving about in the field.
Flash Harriet stopped and pointed at a group beside
the closest hut.

Two of them were sitting down on their nests and five
of them were standing in a circle. As Flash Harriet
watched, three ostriches pushed two fatter ones out
of the way.

"I've got a funny feeling about those fatter ostriches," whispered Flash Harriet.

"They all the look the same to me," said Greta Gloop.

Flash Harriet sighed. "Remember what I said about the raisins."

Two minutes later, Flash Harriet and Greta Gloop pushed their way through the ostriches to look into the nest. It was empty.

An ostrich sidled up to Flash Harriet.

"I've got the eggs," said a man's voice. "Let's go."

Flash Harriet's heart went THUMP! She was standing beside the thieves! She threw a handful of raisins as far away from the nest as possible. Immediately all the ostriches galloped off to eat them, leaving the two thieves behind.

"NOW!" shouted Flash Harriet at the top of her voice.

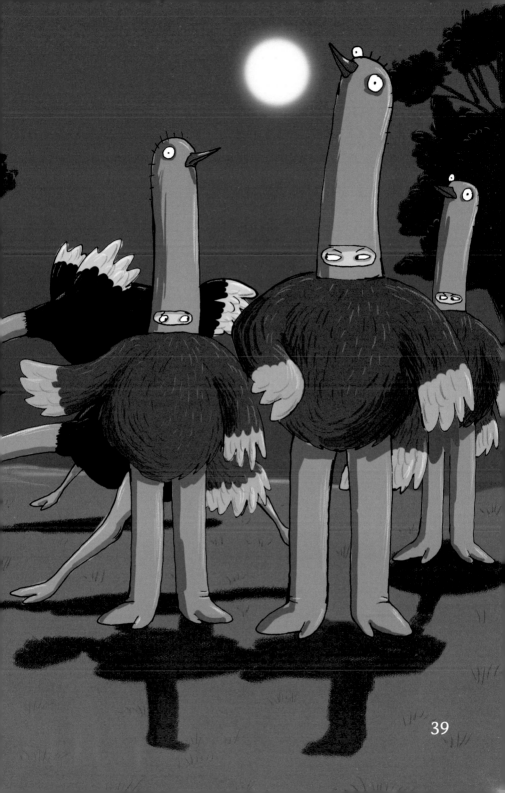

Everything happened at once!

As Greta Gloop pulled off the tops of the thieves'
costumes, Barnaby Fuddle switched on a spotlight
fixed on the roof of the hut exactly where Flash Harriet
had asked him to put it. She pulled out her camera.

SNAP! SNAP! SNAP!

The two thieves stood frozen like statues on the spot. They both had shark faces and slicked-back hair!

Flash Harriet was right!

The thieves were Colin and Nigel Grabbit and they were identical twins!

Barnaby Fuddle jumped down from the roof. He was carrying the rope that Flash Harriet had asked him to bring. The next minute, the Grabbit brothers were tied up like two leeks in a bunch.

"I hate you," snarled Colin Grabbit, who was still wearing his pink shirt. "It was you who wanted the money."

"No, I didn't," yelled Nigel.

"Yes, you did," shouted Colin.

A van roared up the lane and two police officers got out.

"Wait!" Flash Harriet held up her hand and fixed the thieves with a hard stare. "Where are the missing eggs?"

"In the boot of the limousine," muttered Colin Grabbit. He turned to his brother. "It was his idea."

"No, it wasn't!" yelled Nigel.

"Yes, it was!" shouted Colin.

Then they were bundled into the van and taken away.

"Good riddance to bad rubbish," said Greta Gloop.

Barnaby Fuddle whooped with delight and danced about.

"Flash Harriet!" he cried. "You caught the thieves! Now my eggs are safe, I can afford to keep my farm! How can I thank you?"

"Easy!" Flash Harried grinned. "How about a crate of *Ostrich Delight* and a truckload of eggs?"

"Consider it done!" cried Barnaby Fuddle. He punched the air with his fists. "Flash Harriet is the best detective ever!"

44

45

Flash Harriet solves the puzzle

1 Barnaby Fuddle's ostrich eggs are being stolen and he's running out of money.

2 Barnaby has borrowed money from the bank, and the shark-faced bank manager wants it back.

3 When Flash Harriet keeps watch, she doesn't see anyone take the ostrich eggs, but they still disappear.

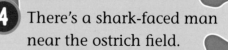

4 There's a shark-faced man near the ostrich field.

5 There's a shark-faced property developer called Colin Grabbit.

6 The fancy dress company says ostrich suits have been very popular recently.

7 The shark-faced bank manager is called Nigel Grabbit.

8 Only real ostriches like raisins.

47

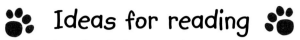

Ideas for reading

Written by Linda Pagett B.Ed (hons), M.Ed
Lecturer and Educational Consultant

Learning objectives: interrogate texts to deepen understanding; identify and summarise evidence from a text; deduce characters' reasons for behaviour from their actions; explain how writers use figurative and expressive language to create images and atmosphere; create roles showing how behaviour can be interpreted from different viewpoints

Curriculum links: Citizenship

Interest words: ostrich, composer, tarantula, limousine, niggling, investment, tricycle

Resources: paper, pens, ICT

Getting started

This book can be read over two or more reading sessions.

- Check that children know what ostriches are and ask children to describe them to the group. Has anyone seen any ostriches before?

- Introduce the book by inviting one of the children to read the blurb on front and back covers. Ask them to predict who might be stealing the eggs and why.

Reading and responding

- Demonstrate reading pp2–5 and then ask the children what they have learnt about Flash Harriet and her family. What clues are there that she might make a good detective?

- Ask children to read to the end of the book, making notes of any clues they think will be useful to working out the final outcome.

- Listen to weaker readers, prompting and praising for appropriate strategies, e.g. well-informed guessing of unfamiliar words, re-reading difficult sentences.